Contents

3 8043 69562380 7

For Hannah

First published in 2013 in Great Britain by
Barrington Stoke Ltd
18 Walker Street, Edinburgh, EH3 7LP

www.barringtonstoke.co.uk

ISBN: 978-1-78112-202-0

Printed in China by Leo

Chapter 1
The Magic Mirror

Look.

How many times do I have to say this?

No one ever seems to get it, so I will repeat it yet again.

I never wanted the stupid mirror in the first place!

The mirror was a present from my new husband, King Frank. We hadn't been married very long, and he was still at the stage where he was happy to spend money on me. I really wanted shoes, but Frank didn't take the hint. Not even when I left the catalogue open at the right page with a big cross next to the red high heels.

The mirror was gift-wrapped. I tore off the ribbons, ripped off the paper and held it up. I didn't like the size, or the shape, or the frame, or the chain. In fact, I didn't like anything about it. The glass reflected my unimpressed face.

"It's *magic*, darling," Frank explained. He was beaming. So pleased with himself for coming up with such a wonderful idea.

Huh.

"I sent away for it," he told me. "You look into it and say a little rhyme and it tells you how beautiful you are."

Now, I know I'm beautiful. I don't need to be told. And I know a thing or two about magic as well. I'm highly skilled in witchcraft, but of course Frank doesn't know that. I've got a Seeing Pool in my secret lair down in the castle dungeons. It's state of the art and it tells me everything I want to know. The lair is also where I keep my bottles of poison, my chest of disguises and some other stuff I'd rather Frank didn't know about.

So I don't need a Magic Mirror. Besides, they are so last year.

"What's the rhyme?" I asked. I couldn't care less, but it was clear that Frank was dying to see how it worked.

"It's written on a card tucked in the back of the frame," Frank said. "Go on, darling. Give it a go."

I tried not to yawn as I turned the mirror over and found the stupid card.

"Read it out, then," Frank pleaded. He was really excited.

"*Mirror, mirror, here I stand,*" I read. "*Who is the fairest in the land?*"

The mirror did a swirly thing that made me feel a bit ill. Then a big, green face appeared. It was some sort of ghastly Genie. He had horns on his head and a ring in his nose. I didn't take to him at all.

Frank was really impressed. His eyes boggled. It was his first taste of magic.

The Genie leered at me and said, "*You, O Queen, are the fairest in the land.*" Then with a pop he vanished, and my own unimpressed face swam back into view.

That was it. Pathetic. It didn't even rhyme. Also, the Genie had a silly voice that didn't go with his looks. Sort of high and squeaky. Annoying.

"Amazing, eh?" Frank cried. "What do you think? Do you like it, darling? It was very, *very* expensive. But only the best for you!"

"Thank you," I said. "It's a very – um – kind gift, Frank."

Just then, Snow White skipped into the room. She's my step-daughter. Frank adores her, but I'm not keen.

"Good morning, Daddy Dearest," said Snow White. She threw herself into her father's lap and showered his beard with kisses. Then she turned to me. "Good morning, Step-mother," she said. "Isn't it a lovely day?"

"It is, my love," said Frank. "What do you plan to do this fine morning?"

"I shall pick some flowers," said Snow White. "And then I shall go and play with my friends, the forest animals. I do love them so. But first, I shall sing you a little song I made up about bunnies. It's got a dance that goes with it."

"Isn't she wonderful?" Frank asked me. "So sweet. So pretty. So talented. So – "

"Mm," I said. "Well, I must be off. I'm going to the shops." And I stormed from the room before I said something unwise. Behind me, Snow White skipped around, pointing her toes and singing some drippy song about bunny rabbits hopping in the sunshine.

"Don't forget your mirror, darling!" Frank called after me.

"Tell a servant to put it up in my bedroom," I snapped. If the truth be told, I would rather it went down the well.

I ordered up the golden coach and went out for the day. I bought two new coats, four pairs of shoes, six dresses, a ruby ring with earrings to match, and nine handbags. I went to Boots and topped up on lipstick, nail varnish and poison. I also treated myself to coffee and cake at the best hotel in town. The macaroons were to die for.

I enjoyed myself. It was good to get away from Snow White for the day. There is only so much of her that I can take.

Chapter 2
My Evil Plan

"You never use that Magic Mirror I gave you, darling," Frank said, a week or so later. We were in the breakfast hall, drinking coffee.

"Yes, I do, darling," I said. "I used it a few days ago."

"And what did it say?" Frank asked.

"Nothing new. It's very limited."

"You mean you don't like it?" Frank sounded rather sad. I didn't want to upset him. In fact, I needed to keep him sweet. The bill for my massive shopping spree would arrive any day.

"Oh no, darling," I purred. "I love it. In fact, I'll go up and use it right now."

Outside the window, I saw Snow White run across the lawn in a cloud of song-birds and butterflies. She had a baby rabbit in her arms and a small deer trotted at her heels. She was coming for her morning hug-in with daddy.

I was glad of an excuse to get out.

I went up to my room and marched over to the mirror on the wall. I gave a sigh and said the rubbishy little rhyme.

"*Mirror, mirror, here I stand. Who is the fairest in the land?*"

I tapped my foot and waited. There was the usual sick-making swirly effect, and the Genie appeared. He had a glint in his yellow eye that I didn't like. He smacked his lips and gave a titter.

He said, "*You, O Queen, are the fairest here, but Snow White is a thousand times more fair.*" And he vanished, with a smirk.

Now, that was a shock! I can tell you I wasn't expecting that. Oh, she's all right, I suppose, with her hair-as-black-as-ebony and lips-as-red-as-blood and silly little teeth-as-white-as-snow. But a thousand times fairer than me? I don't *think* so.

I'll admit I was upset. *More* than upset. Hopping mad, in fact. I brooded about it all day. At tea time, I didn't say a word. I just watched as Snow White chattered away, buttering dainty little pieces of bread and babbling on about the tame fox that's taken to following her

around. She calls it Mr Bushybrush. Frank, as always, was enchanted.

"Mr Bushybrush?" he kept crying. "Mr Bushybrush? Ho, ho, ho! My word, what a lovely, funny name. Did you hear that, darling? Snow White's fox is called Mr Bushybrush. How does she come up with it? What a clever little poppet you are, my love."

I had to get up and leave. To my mind, Mr Bushybrush is a wet name to call a fox. If I had a pet fox, I would call it Killer. To make matters worse, Snow White had a new dress on and was looking even prettier than usual.

"Don't you want more coffee, darling?" Frank called after me.

"NO!" I snapped, and went down into my lair to brood and mix poison. Mixing poison always calms me down.

That night, I didn't sleep a wink. I lay awake and plotted.

I had to come up with a plan to get rid of Snow White. I don't like competitors when it comes to looks. It takes a lot of effort and money to keep myself looking young and beautiful, and she doesn't even have to try.

Besides, the girl was obsessed with animals. The horrid creatures followed her everywhere. There were hairs on the throne cushions and stains on the carpets. You had to check before you sat down, in case of fleas, fur balls or hibernating hedgehogs. Song-birds had made a nest in the candelabra above the dinner table. I found droppings in the sugar bowl. It was not healthy.

By the time morning came, I had a plan all worked out. I would send for the chief huntsman and command him to take her into the forest and dispose of her.

Harsh, I know. But I don't mess about.

The huntsman wasn't keen. He pointed out that disposing of little girls wasn't in his job spec. Besides, he would feel mean.

I said, "Get over it. Do as I say, or you won't have a job at all."

He said, "I don't know ... Little Snow White. Such a pretty little thing."

"Yes, well," I snapped. "You're welcome to your opinion. Oh, and this deal is between you and me. You'll have to keep your mouth shut about it. And do it tonight."

He said, "How much are you paying?"

I said, "How does a purse of gold sound?"

He said, "Sounds good."

I said, "I'll want proof, of course. That you've disposed of her."

He said, "What sort of proof?"

I said, "Her heart should do it. Take a paper bag. Bring it to me the second you return."

He said, "Do I get paid now?"

"No. Heart first, gold later."

He shook his head and walked off, muttering.

I don't know. You just can't get the staff.

Chapter 3
Surprise

The next morning, I skipped breakfast. If all had gone well and the huntsman had carried out my orders, Snow White was a goner. I didn't want to deal with Frank's fuss and bother when she didn't appear for their morning cuddle.

I went straight to the huntsman's house on the edge of the palace grounds. I pushed open the door and walked in. He was sitting with his head in his hands, looking glum.

"Did you do it?" I asked.

He nodded.

I said, "Well? Where's the heart?"

He pointed at the dresser. There was a soggy-looking paper bag on the shelf. I reached for it.

"Not that one," said the huntsman. "That's my dinner for tonight. It's mince. What you want is in the drawer."

It *was* in the drawer. Yuck. I took one look and made up my mind I wouldn't take it back to the palace. I didn't want it to leak all over the rugs.

"Put it in the bin," I said. "And remember – not one word. Here's your reward."

I held out a fat purse. I'd been through Frank's trouser pockets for loose gold. There was rather a lot.

That cheered the huntsman up.

I rushed back to the palace and ran up the stairs to my room. For once, I couldn't wait to use the magic mirror.

I said the rhyme. *"Mirror, mirror, here I stand. Who is the fairest in the land?"*

The glass wobbled and swirled and the Genie appeared. He looked pleased with himself, like he knew something I didn't.

He said,

"You, O Queen, are the fairest here,
But Snow White, who has gone to stay
With seven dwarfs, far, far away
Is a thousand times more fair."

He was about to vanish, but I stopped him just in time.

"Hold it right there!" I said,

He stopped and said, "What?"

I said, "Are you sure about that?"

He said, "Yes. That's the rhyme."

I said, "It doesn't rhyme. Poetry is not your thing. But that's not the point. What was that you said about dwarfs?"

"I'll say it again, if I must," said the Genie. *"You, O Queen, are the fair –"*

"Never mind," I said. "It'll be faster to find out myself. I've got a Seeing Pool down in the lair – I'll use that. Now, buzz off."

I rushed down to my lair and made straight for the Seeing Pool. A Seeing Pool is pretty much just a garden pond with extra magical features.

I stuck a finger in the water and said, "Show me Snow White! Hurry!" Then I waited for the ripples to settle.

When they did, I couldn't believe what I saw!

The Genie was right.

Snow White was far from dead. She was alive and kicking, and had indeed set up house in the forest with seven dwarfs! Their house was a small cottage with a crooked chimney, set in a leafy glade.

So the huntsman had lied to me! He must have taken pity on her and let her go. Goodness knows what was in his drawer. It had *looked* like a heart. He must have got it from the butcher, when he got the mince.

I was tempted to go straight back and shout at him, but I couldn't tear myself away from the pool. I watched Snow White blow kisses as the dwarfs set off for what turned out to be the local diamond mine. I watched them dig for a bit, but it was so incredibly boring that I switched back to Snow White.

I ordered the Pool to show me inside the cottage. Snow White was making beds and sweeping the floor. The usual collection of birds and animals were helping her. She looked perfectly happy and healthy. Arrgh! What a disaster!

I wondered how she had got on, all alone in the forest at night. Fine, I bet. After all, she had all her little forest friends to protect her. They had probably led her to the cottage.

It seemed that my work was far from done. What should I do now?

My eye fell on my chest of disguises.

Chapter 4
I Visit the Cottage

A few hours later, I stood outside the dwarfs' cottage with a tray of pretty things. I was dressed up as a ragged old peddler woman, with a floppy hat and hoop earrings. I was confident that Snow White wouldn't recognise me.

"Pretty things for sale!" I cried, in an old-woman voice. "For sale! Pretty things!"

Snow White poked her head out of the window and said, "Good day, old woman. What have you got?"

"Nice things," I said. "Nice, pretty things. Ribbons, all colours."

"I'll be right there," Snow White trilled.

A moment later, the door opened and out she came.

"Look at this," I said. "A lovely pink ribbon. Just your colour. Let me thread it in your dress, my dear. Turn round."

She turned her back to me and I threaded the ribbon. Then I pulled.

"It's a bit tight," said Snow White.

I pulled even harder.

"I can't breathe!" gasped Snow White. "I can't – ah – "

And she collapsed on the ground. I couldn't see any sign of breathing.

Result!

I didn't hang about. I climbed on my broomstick, which I'd parked behind a bush, and flew back to the palace. I felt a lot more cheerful. Frank hadn't even noticed that I'd gone. He was out organising the staff, who were searching all over the grounds for Snow White. He looked almost frantic with worry.

I hid the broomstick in a hedge and sneaked past. No one saw me. I rushed up to the bedroom, changed back into my queen's robes and stood before the mirror. I said the rhyme and waited for the Genie.

Imagine my surprise and irritation when he repeated word for word the same stupid remarks that he had made that morning.

"How is that possible?" I snapped. "She *was* living with seven dwarfs, but I've just been there and done away with her!"

"Ah, but she wasn't dead," said the Genie. "She only fainted. The dwarfs came back and took off the ribbon and she's fine again. You did a rotten job. What's more, the dwarfs suspected it was you and made her promise not to open the door to strangers any more. So you won't catch her out again that easy."

I said, "Want a bet?" And I stormed off back down to my lair. I'm not used to not getting my own way. This time, Snow White really had it coming.

I mixed poisons until I felt better. Then I had another rummage through my chest of disguises. I was tempted by the gorilla suit, but decided against it. Even an animal lover like Snow White would think twice before opening the door to a gorilla.

In the end, I went for the old woman disguise again, but with a head scarf. I changed the make up, too. I gave myself rosy cheeks and padded myself out with a lot of woolly cardigans and shawls. I even had a different tray, with different stuff. No ribbons this time. Just a range of fans, some necklaces and a few pairs of cheap gloves.

Oh – and a poisoned comb! It was large and green. I put it in pride of place on the tray.

I examined my reflection in the Seeing Pool. Excellent. My own mother wouldn't know me.

It was too late to go back that day. The dwarfs would be home. I would put all the stuff into a sack and take it up to my bedroom. Then I'd have an early night and set off at first light in the morning.

Chapter 5
My Second Visit

"Different pretty things for sale!" I called, from the doorstep. "For sale!"

There was a pause. Then Snow White looked out of the window.

"I'm not allowed to come out," she said.

"And why is that, my pretty?" I asked.

"Because yesterday, a wicked old woman tried to hurt me. My friends the dwarfs only just saved me in time. They think she was my step-mother in disguise."

"Really?" I said. "That's the worst thing I've ever heard. Why would anyone want to hurt a nice girl like you?"

"Anyway," said Snow White "I'm not allowed to come out."

"I understand," I said. "You can't be too careful. But you can look, can't you?"

"Oh yes," she said. "I suppose there's no harm in looking."

"Do you see the fans?" I said. "And the lovely necklaces? And just look at this beautiful green comb. Just pop your head out the window, and I'll comb your hair for you."

The second the comb touched her head, she collapsed again. Really. The girl has no sense at all.

I congratulated myself as I flew back to the castle. The gardeners were dragging the lake and checking all the outhouses. It seems that Frank was in a state of collapse. Not only was his darling Snow White missing, but the bill for my shopping spree had arrived.

As soon as I had changed, I spoke with the mirror again. This time I was sure I would get the correct answer.

But no! Believe it or not, those rotten dwarfs had come home, found her and pulled out the comb. They had given her a herbal remedy and another long lecture about not trusting anyone. The Genie was thrilled to tell me all the details.

Foiled again!

I was getting fed up with this. Fed up of all the disguises and the comings and goings and having to put up with the Genie, who seemed to enjoy his role as bringer of bad news far too much.

I decided to try again a third time – and this time, I would pull out all the stops.

Yet again, I opened my trusty chest. This time, I went for a long, hooded cloak. Instead of a tray, I chose a basket. Instead of ribbons and combs and the like, I would appeal to her greed. I would take along a basket full of apples. I knew she liked those.

Now, this was the clever bit. I would poison one of the apples. Not all of it. Just one half. If I could trick her into eating it, my work would at last be done.

The next morning, there I was again outside the dwarfs' cottage.

"Apples!" I cried. "Fresh, rosy apples!"

"Go away, please," came Snow White's voice from inside. "I'm not buying anything today!"

"But I've got apples," I called. "Fresh picked this morning. Come to the window, young miss, and I'll show you."

She came to the window, which was closed tight. She shook her head and waved at me to tell me to go away.

I said, "Open up, dearie, and I'll make you a present of one."

She said, "No. I'm not allowed to take anything."

"Why not?"

"Because someone might have done something bad to it. It might be poisoned."

"Rubbish!" I chuckled. "What a silly little thing you are. I'll cut it in half. See? I'll eat the green side and you can have the red half. Look, you can watch me do it."

I sliced the apple in half with a knife, and took a huge bite of the green side.

"Yum, yum," I said. "Ooh. This is some apple, this is. So juicy."

Snow White watched me eat it. I could see she was tempted.

"You see?" I called. "Nothing wrong with it. It's harmless. Open the window just a crack, and I'll pass in your half."

Squeak, went the window. *Crunch* went the apple as she bit into it.

Thunk! That was her hitting the deck. She wouldn't get up this time. That apple had enough poison in to floor an elephant.

"Cheerio, Snow White," I crowed. "I don't think we'll meet again."

And off I flew, back to the palace, where I once again stood in front of the mirror.

This time, I got the result I wanted. The Genie nearly choked as he uttered the words I longed to hear.

"You, O Queen, are the fairest in the land."

Music to my ears!

Chapter 6
Arguments

I was looking forward to life without Snow White, but things didn't work out the way I planned. In the main this was because of Frank.

He was obsessed with finding his missing daughter. He ordered posters to be put up all over the kingdom. He sent out town criers. He offered a huge reward for information.

He was so grumpy that I could never be bothered to talk to him. Not that he had anything interesting to say to me anyway. He was too busy whining about Snow White.

I came down to breakfast one day to find him weeping into his porridge. Again.

"Good day," I said. "Lovely morning."

"Oh, Snow White!" he moaned. "My little Snow White! Where is she?"

"I'm sorry but I haven't a clue," I said. "Pass the marmalade."

"How I miss her!" he wailed. "How I long for a sight of her pretty face. What shall I do without her?"

"Finish your porridge, for a start," I said. "It's getting cold."

"How can I think of eating?" he sobbed. "She could be starving in a hedge somewhere."

"Indeed," I said. "Do you want that last piece of toast, or shall I have it?"

"I don't care about toast!" Frank roared. "And I do think you could show a bit more pity for me."

"Oh, I do pity you, darling," I said. "It's just that I need a good breakfast because I'm off to the shops. I might be out all day."

"The shops?" snapped Frank. "Surely you're not going to the shops *again*? How many more clothes do you need? I've only just settled the bill for your last trip."

"I am the Queen," I reminded him. "I'm supposed to look nice. After all, I'm the fairest in the land. I like to dress the part."

"Perhaps," said Frank. He sounded rather cold. "Perhaps. But you're costing me a fortune. I shall be shelling out a great deal of money for the reward when my darling Snow White returns."

"*If* she returns," I said. It slipped out before I could stop myself.

"What are you saying?" asked Frank.

"Well, she ran away, didn't she?" I said. "That might mean she wasn't happy here. She might prefer to stay where she is happy." I helped myself to a muffin. "Mmm. These are rather nice."

"She didn't run away!" roared Frank. "Why would she run away from her daddy, who loves her? It's clear she has been kidnapped."

"Or eaten by bears," I said. Oops. That was the wrong thing to say.

"Bears!" Frank wailed. "Oh, no! Bears! How could you even think such a terrible thing?"

"I'm just being practical," I said. "Do stop being such a baby, Frank. She's gone. Deal with it."

"Cruel!" he gasped. "You are a cruel woman with a cold heart! I sometimes wish I had never married you!"

He got up and stormed out of the room. I was left to finish the last of the muffins.

I stayed out of his way over the next week. I ate my meals in my room. Out of spite, I went to the shops every day. If there's one thing I cannot stand, it is meanness. So I ordered myself a whole new wardrobe. I chose new carpets to replace the ones Snow White's animals had destroyed. I replaced my broomstick and treated myself to a fabulous set of designer suitcases that cost more than a small house.

I threw the mirror in the bin. I wouldn't be needing that again.

Chapter 7
The Letter

A number of times, I tried to seek out the huntsman. I wanted to confront him about letting Snow White go, and to take back the purse of gold. But any time I went to his house, he was never in.

I had just returned from yet another failed trip, when something happened that I didn't see coming. The postman was walking down the path with a jolly whistle. We didn't speak. I'm the Queen. I don't talk to postmen.

I was creeping past the breakfast hall, trying to avoid Frank, when I heard a sudden cry.

"She's alive!" Frank shouted. "Oh, joy! My darling is alive!"

What was this? I turned back and threw open the door.

"What?" I said. "Did I hear you speak?"

His happy face changed when he saw me. He went white with fury. He had a letter in his hand. He held it out to me.

"Read this," he snarled. "Read it, you wicked woman!"

I took the letter. It was written on fancy paper. This is what it said.

Dearest Daddy,

I hope you haven't been too worried. A lot has happened over the last two weeks. I hope you won't be upset at what I have to tell you.

Daddy darling, Step-mother has been trying to kill me. She asked the huntsman to do it, but he let me go. Then my dear animal friends led me to a sweet little house in the forest where seven kind dwarfs took me in.

Step-mother found out and tried to kill me three times. I was a little bit silly, but you know I always trust people. The first two times, the dwarfs saved me. The third time, she gave me a poisoned apple and they thought I was dead for sure. They put me in a glass coffin on top of a hill, and sat by it day and night.

Then — would you believe it — a prince came riding by. He asked if he could take me back to his castle, and put me in a special room, with organ music and fancy candles. The dwarfs agreed but when they lifted the coffin, the piece of apple in my mouth fell out. Lo and behold, I came to! Wasn't I lucky?

The prince is very nice. He is called Leopold. He is very handsome, with lovely curly hair. We have fallen in love and are going to be married. I am very happy, and look forward to seeing you at the wedding.

Sorry to have caused such a fuss.

Lots of love,
Your little Snow White.

Oops.

"So!" roared Frank. "What do you have to say for yourself?"

Well, there wasn't much I *could* say, was there? It was a fair cop.

I threw the letter down and stormed from the room. Then I went upstairs to pack. It's a good thing I bought the designer suitcases.

There are plenty more kings in the world. Time to move on.

Our books are tested
for children and young people by
children and young people.

Thanks to everyone who consulted on
a manuscript for their time and effort in
helping us to make our books better
for our readers.

*Also by **Kaye Umanksy**...*

The Wickedest Witch in the World

Old Maggit reckons she's got just the ticket to win the Wickedest Witch Contest. A house of sweets to tempt the kiddies in and a big oven to roast them!

But Maggit was planning on catching some nice, well-behaved children. She didn't expect a pair of brats with an attitude problem. It's a case for Supernanny, but Maggit will just have to do!

This is *Hansel and Gretel* as you've never read it before.

The Stepsisters' Story

Move over Cinders –
the Stepsisters are here!

Lardine and Angula have their sights set on the Prince. No stupid servant's going to stand in their way...

This is *Cinderella*
as you've never read it before.

www.barringtonstoke.co.uk